WELSH TALES FOR THE FIRESIDE

WELSH TALES
FOR THE FIRESIDE

LISA LEE

GOMER

First Publication — 1998

ISBN 1 85902 542 0

Printed in Wales at
Gomer Press, Llandysul, Ceredigion

CONTENTS

The first three stories and 'Iorwerth and the Pet Lamb' were published in *Owen's Story Book* (Wilding & Son Ltd., 1955), and were illustrated by Reginald Woolley. The author and publishers gratefully acknowledge permission given by the author's sister, Mrs Iris Joyce, to reproduce them here. 'The Pepper Pot Office' and 'The Post Office Badger' appeared in *Owen's Second Story Book* (Wilding & Son Ltd., 1962). The new illustrations are by Robin Lawrie.

THE LUCKY FISHMONGER

Once upon a time not so very long ago, old Dwalad
the fisherman lived in a cottage on the shores of Lake
Tegid. It was a whitewashed cottage facing the
mountains at the end of the lake, and old Dwalad lived
there alone with his dog, Jim.

He was the best and most famous fisherman in all
that part of Wales. He fished in the river that ran
through the lake, and in the river that joined it by the
old bridge. But more often he rowed out into the
middle of the lake in his old, grey boat and caught
trout and pike and perch, and sometimes in the stream

trout and pike and perch, and sometimes in the stream of river water, a salmon.

Old Dwalad's skin was brown as a berry and he had a soft slow voice and clear blue eyes, and Jim the dog was black and white, and had once been very good with the sheep. They lived very happily together, though they were very poor. Ordinary travellers who crossed the mountains to visit the village and the beautiful lake did not believe that Dwalad knew the exact place where the river waters ran, nor did they believe the tales told of the old city that lay drowned and ruined under the waters of the lake. But old Dwalad, whose mother was a gipsy, was very wise and understood all these things.

One late spring morning, when the weather was just right for fishing, Old Dwalad left his cottage and whistled up his dog.

'Well, Jim, my boy, this is a lovely day for salmon, and I'm off to try and get a big one.'

The dog rushed, barking joyfully, out of the gate and followed the old fisherman down to the landing stage and waited while he untied his boat and got ready to leave. Then he ran back to the cottage. He would be waiting at the landing stage to meet him when he returned.

And old Dwalad rowed out into the lake and fished until noon; he did not see a fish at all, but was quite happy watching the water. Then he ate a packet of sandwiches and prepared to fish again. The only fish he saw all afternoon was a gwyniad, and he knew that even he could not catch that. He began to think that perhaps this was not such a good day after all, when a squall came up from the west and whipped up the waters of the lake so that they were grey and angry. So old Dwalad decided to row home and, just at that unlikely moment, he hooked a fish. He knew that it was a big one by the way his rod bent over, and soon he saw it fling itself out of the water. But Dwalad knew all the tricks, and the fish did not stand a chance against his skill, and though it thrashed about and fought, it was not long before it was safely landed in the boat.

And as Dwalad turned to row home, a flash of lightning tore the sky and almost at the same moment there was a clap of thunder. Knowing the storm was right overhead, Dwalad rowed home as fast as he could. The rain was coming down like pennies, but when he got to the landing stage Jim was not there waiting for him.

'I expect he is afraid of the storm,' thought Dwalad, as he walked home proudly with the huge fish.

When he got into the kitchen of his cottage, he called, 'Jim, Jim,' but the dog only barked and growled and wouldn't come out from his box under the kitchen table.

'Look,' said the old fisherman, 'look at the splendid salmon that I've caught'; but the dog wouldn't come out and ran snarling into the bedroom and lay whining under the bed.

So Dwalad just thought that the storm had upset him, and took a large knife from the drawer in the dresser and slit open the fish, and there, lying in its stomach, he found a great gold ring. It was no ordinary ring, but made of the finest gold and very heavy, and it was engraved all over with fishes' heads. Dwalad had never seen anything like it in all his long life. He laughed and put the ring on his finger and called again to his dog.

'Look, Jim bach, look! I have found a great gold ring in this fish's stomach. I will go across the mountains to Dinas Mawddwy and sell it to a dealer, and we will be rich for the rest of our lives.'

But the dog only snarled and howled, and there was another flash of lightning and a growl of thunder.

So Dwalad put the ring on a shelf over the fireplace and put on a fish kettle to boil. Then he ran out into his garden and picked a bunch of herbs, and put the fish on to cook. He let it boil for five minutes and pushed it on to the side of the stove to cool all night. Then he ate some bread and cheese, lit his pipe and his candles, took his Bible from the shelf, and started to read a chapter from the book of the prophet Isaiah, before going to bed.

It was a wild and stormy night, and the rain beat on the windows and the wind rattled the old doors and howled in the chimney. And just as the hands of the clock on the mantelpiece reached nine o'clock, someone came to the cottage door and knocked once.

'Who is there?' said old Dwalad; but no one answered.

'Who is there?' he said again. But still no one spoke, so he went and opened the door—but there was no one there, only the black and noisy night; and there was nothing to show that anyone had been there save for the mark of a little wet hand on the door. So Dwalad shut the door, put away his Bible and went to bed.

Next day was terribly cold and windy and no good for fishing at all so Dwalad stayed in making trout flies out of pheasants' feathers, and when evening came he sat by the fire and lit his candles and took out his pipe to have a smoke before going to bed.

And the storm still blew, and the rain lashed against the windows and the wind shook the cottage and howled in the chimney, and as the old clock struck nine, someone came to the cottage door and knocked twice.

'Who's there?' said the old fisherman, and Jim the dog barked angrily. 'Who is there?' But no one answered; so old Dwalad went and opened the door, but there was no one out there in the storm, and there was nothing to show that anyone had been there but for the mark of two little wet feet on the doorstep.

Dwalad came in and shut the door.

'Whoever has come to my house twice,' he said, 'will come three times, and if it is the last thing I do, I will see him and speak to him, and ask him what he wants of me.'

And for the first time in his life, he locked his front door. Then he blew out the candles and went to bed; but he did not sleep very well that night, and neither did his dog.

And next day he went out into the garden and picked a bunch of strange herbs—basil, rue, garlic and hyssop—and these he hung over the front door. Then he sat and waited for what should come to his door at nine. He did not light his candles, but sat in the firelight. And just as the old clock whirred and prepared to strike, he went and looked out of the window and flung open the door. Suddenly the stormy night was filled with a strange and beautiful blue light rather like moonlight. Then round the corner of the cottage came the most beautiful little girl that Dwalad had ever seen. She was dressed in a silvery dress that shone like the stars, her hair was the palest gold, and her eyes were bluer than the sea. But she was crying, and her tears rolled down her cheeks like great diamonds.

'Give me back my ring,' she cried. 'Give me back my ring.'

'Who are you,' said Dwalad, 'and how do you know that I have got your ring?'

'You are Cadwaladr Edwards,' she said, 'and you went out three days ago and caught a salmon in the lake that had swallowed my ring. Give it to me back, please give it to me back.'

'It is true,' said the old man, 'that I am Cadwaladr Edwards, though how you know this I cannot say, and it is true that I have a ring, but it would be far too big for your little hand.'

'I know, I know; it is my father's ring that I must wear when I grow up,' said the little girl. 'I lost it while I was playing with my brothers and sisters, and my father is very angry, and I cannot go back to my palace under the lake unless you give me back my ring. Please give it to me.'

'Why should I do this thing?' said old Dwalad. 'I am an old man; I have worked hard all my life, and I am still very poor. If I take this ring, which you say is yours, and sell it over the pass at Dinas, I shall have a little comfort in my old age for myself and my dog.'

Then the little girl said, 'If you give me back my ring, you will catch so many fish that you will have to hire a man to help you sell it, and then you will open a shop, and travellers will come over the mountains and buy fish from you.'

'Few travellers pass this way, the roads are too dangerous,' said old Dwalad.

'They will build a great new road from England,' said the little girl. 'You will be very rich.'

13

'I do not believe you,' said old Dwalad. 'I prefer to keep the ring.'

Then the little girl clenched her fists and her eyes blazed blue fire, and she cried, 'When I am in the water I am a good spirit; but when I am out of the water I am an evil spirit, and I will do evil to you and yours if you do not give me back my ring.'

'Do your worst,' said the old fisherman. 'I do not fear you.'

Then there was a blinding flash of lightning and old Dwalad blinked, and when he opened his eyes again the little girl had disappeared, but the bunch of herbs over the door was burned and blackened. So he went back indoors and put the kettle on, and though he waited a long time, the water would not boil; and a copper saucepan fell off the mantelshelf and hit him on the head. Then he went to his larder to fetch some of the salmon for his supper, but he found that the fish had gone bad, so he went sadly to bed, hungry, and called his dog; but the dog would not come, and that made Dwalad more unhappy, as Jim was really his best friend.

Next morning, when he woke up, he tried to pretend that the whole thing had been a bad dream, and took his boat out on to the lake, and tried to fish. But he fished all day and caught nothing, and then the boat sprung a leak, and he only just got to the landing stage in time.

So next day he determined to be rid of the ring and take it over the mountains to Dinas Mawddwy and sell it.

It was a long walk by the shores of the lake and up a very steep and rough road to the pass, so Dwalad started off early. He put on his oilskins and an old hat, and left the dog in the garden. It was a wild, grey day, and anyone sensible would have stayed at home, but Dwalad was determined to set out, and even though a slate blew off the roof and narrowly missed his head, he struggled down his little garden path and opened his gate. As he shut the gate the hinge came away from the post, and the gate fell down, and Dwalad knew that by the time he got home the sheep from the farm would be in his garden, nibbling all his young vegetables. But he just buttoned up his coat and went on.

The lake looked cold and angry, the colour of a dark slate with small white horses on it, and there were no mountains to be seen at the end as the clouds had come right down. Dwalad struggled on against the wind along the five miles on the shores of the lake, and then, as the track turned up towards the mountain, he saw that a large branch from an oak tree had fallen across the road and no one could pass. So he stopped and helped a farmer that he knew to clear a way through.

'Where are you off to, Dwalad, on a day like this?' asked the farmer.

'Dinas. . .' said Dwalad, suddenly wondering why.

'Dinas, man?' said the farmer. 'You'll be lucky if the road isn't washed away after all this rain.'

But Dwalad just smiled and set his face towards the long steep climb up to Bwlch-y-groes. The road here wound round like an overhanging shelf before it reached the summit of the pass, and plunged eighteen hundred feet down the other side to Llan-y-Mawddwy.

Poor old Dwalad was very much out of breath when he reached the last sheep gate before the precipice. And then he saw what he had most feared: the stones and shale had been washed down from the mountain by a swollen waterfall, and they had carried the overhanging road with them, and so that day there was no way through to Dinas Mawddwy.

So poor old Cadwaladr Edwards turned sadly back. 'I am old and tired,' he said to himself. 'Perhaps if I go home and give back this ring to the lake folk, I shall find peace and happiness for myself and my dog, for surely I was never meant to reach the town.'

And as he spoke aloud his thoughts, the sky cleared in the west, and the sun shone with a bright golden light, for it was near evening. And all the mountains got rid of their clouds—the near Arans, Rhobell, and even bad old distant Arenig.

And Dwalad got a lift home in Miss Jones Maes Fedw's dog cart. He sat very quietly, and was very glad that Miss Jones was so deaf so that he did not have to talk. And at his gate, which somebody seemed to have mended, Jim was there barking happily in greeting. and Dwalad went indoors and made a cup of tea.

Then in the twilight evening, under the first star, he rowed out far into the middle of the lake. He sat in his boat and listened and watched the clouds floating away to the mountains in the west. He heard the water lapping gently, and a seagull cry. Then he stood up in the bows of his boat and took the ring from his finger and threw it as far as he could into the lake. The ring skimmed the water like a flat stone and disappeared, and almost at once he heard a voice singing in the air, high and clear and happy, and he knew that all was well.

Then he rowed home and made supper for himself and his dog.

And for days after, he caught so many fish that he was obliged to sell them, and the road from England was mended, and travellers came in great numbers so that Dwalad had to have a boy to help him with the fish. And soon he and the boy and the dog opened a shop in the village, and sold so much fish that they became rich, and Dwalad was known as the lucky fishmonger.

And he and his dog lived happily ever afterwards.

THE SINGING PIGS OF NANT GWYNANT

Once upon a time Maggie and Gwilym-Ifan Evans lived in a farm up above Llyn Gwynant. It was called Coed Uchaf, and looked right across the valley to Snowdon.

Their land was very steep and rough, and there were patches of thorn and scrub where nothing would grow, and which were even too rough for sheep to graze. Gwilym-Ifan had some sheep on the mountain, but his most prized possession was his black sow, Myfanwy.

I am afraid that Maggie and Gwilym-Ifan did not

18

keep a very good farm. Maggie tried very hard, and it probably would have been all right if Gwilym-Ifan had not had such a fine singing voice. In fact, his voice was so good that he was always careering about the countryside on his motor bicycle singing at some test concert or Eisteddfod so that he really did not have time to look after the farm properly. So if it hadn't been for black Myfanwy and her little pigs, I don't know what they would have done. And when Gwilym-Ifan managed to buy an old car it was even worse, for when he took Myfanwy to a farm near Rhyd-ddu to see her husband, Sam, the boar, he used to stop on the way home at the Goat Inn, and sing and shout with his friends, and I am afraid that was where a lot of the money went.

Now Myfanwy was a very clever pig. Gwilym-Ifan did not know this because he had bought her at a sale without looking at her pedigree. Had he looked he would have seen that she was descended from a black sow that had come up out of a lake with a fairy princess.

This fairy princess had married a farmer and then quarrelled with him and had returned to the lake with all her children, belongings and animals. All, that is to say, except Myfanwy's great-great-great-great-great-grandmother who had been out rootling on her own and so missed the trip back to fairyland. So she had had to stay with the mortals, and that is how she came to be related to Myfanwy.

So you see that Myfanwy was really rather a special pig.

She was very inquisitive too, and used to stand with her front feet on the wall of her sty and listen to human conversations and, if it was warm and sunny, she would sometimes fall asleep standing up, and her front trotters would fall off the wall of the sty. She would wake up, grunt, and climb up again. Gradually she learnt that Gwilym-Ifan thought this a very funny trick and would bring his friends out to watch her. And that was how Myfanwy learned so much that was going on.

She admired Gwilym-Ifan's lovely singing voice (as, indeed, did all the ladies), and she always taught all her families to sing. Pig singing cannot be heard by you and me, but it can be heard perfectly by other animals, and it was Myfanwy's beautiful singing that made Sam, her husband, so fond of her.

But there was one song that Myfanwy did not teach her children, and that was, 'This little pig went to market.'

Indeed, she was always very disappointed when Gwilym-Ifan came and took her families off in his trailer, even if they were sometimes getting a bit big and cheeky. And she wondered what she could do to put a stop to this.

Now it happened that the year about which I write was very stormy, and Maggie and Gwilym-Ifan had lost a lot of their sheep in the snow. Myfanwy heard a conversation in the farmhouse kitchen which made her think.

It was a frosty, spring evening, and Gwilym-Ifan had turned the sow loose to chase the hens round the yard, which always made him laugh. Then he went into the house to have his tea before going out to sing somewhere.

Myfanwy stood and scratched her back on the door jamb so that she could listen to the conversation. Mrs. Evans was scolding her husband and telling him not to be back late, telling him that this was a very bad year indeed with the lambs, and that she did not know what they were going to do for money.

'Well,' said Gwilym-Ifan, scratching the sow with a long stick, 'the old sow is going to the boar tomorrow, and we'll have some more piglets in no time to take to market, won't we, cariad?'

And the sow grunted and looked at him with her clever little eyes and thought, 'Oh, no, this time you don't, Gwilym-Ifan Evans. This time I am going to bring up my family myself and have them live with me and look after me in my old age.'

And she squealed and jumped away from the door and ran into the yard and looked up at the brilliant green sky, the thin crescent of the new moon, and the planet Venus pricking the heavens like a bright light showing through a hole in a curtain.

So she was going to see Sam tomorrow; that was

nice, she thought; she was always glad to see dear Sam. And she trotted off down a muddy path and up towards a thorny bit of scrub that ran down to the road. She started to rootle in the ground with her snout and to tear up some of the thorns and brambles. She got so interested in doing this that she did not hear the farmer and his wife calling her. And then she heard the car going rattling down the awful higgledypiggledy farm drive, and she knew it was time for bed.

'Mochyn, Mochyn, Mochyn,' called Maggie, banging an old cake tin, and Myfanwy squealed just for a joke and charged at her, which made Mrs. Evans rather cross so that she drove her across the yard with her stick.

And the sow lay down to sleep and wondered why Gwilym-Ifan did not set his pigs to rootle and clear away all the bramble and thorns on his land so that he could plant potatoes and young trees. And then she went to sleep and snored and snored as pigs do and dreamt about going to see Sam, her husband, to-morrow.

And when she woke up, Gwilym-Ifan was putting her into the trailer and taking her to Rhyd-Ddu. And she spent a lovely afternoon with Sam, and sang to him, and told him all her troubles and they kissed and cuddled as true loves will; and in the evening Gwilym-Ifan came and fetched her. But, as she feared, they drove to the Goat Inn, and poor Myfanwy had to lie in the trailer while Gwilym-Ifan spent a merry evening with his friends, laughing and shouting and singing. And it was very late indeed when they drove up the higgledypiggledy drive and Myfanwy at last went to bed in her sty.

And when the days were warmer and brighter, Myfanwy had five little pigs. She was very happy when they came, and was glad that it was such a small family, for she felt she would get to know them better. They were all black except one, and he was copper coloured with black spots and looked just like a piece of gingerbread with large currants in it.

And the pigs were called Blodwen, Ceinwen, Josephine, Dimple and Ginger, and they were all lady pigs except Ginger. And they were all very gay and happy in the sty, especially Ginger, who dashed about waving his curly tail when he was still very young.

But I am sorry to say that Mrs. and Mr. Evans were far from happy. They were very worried because, you see, they were counting on Myfanwy's having ten or twelve piglets, and now she had only five, they felt she had let them down. Then a worse thing happened. Gwilym-Ifan went out one night in the old car with some friends, and they all got so merry that they drove the car into a telegraph pole on the Llanberis Pass and had to walk home. Maggie was very cross indeed, as Gwilym-Ifan had forgotten to pay the insurance, and they had no money to mend the car. Then he was fined for careless driving and had to pay out a lot of money.

'I fear,' said Gwilym-Ifan one evening as he was passing the pig sty, 'that we shall have to sell the farm.'

Myfanwy was out dozing in the sun, but when she heard that, she woke up quickly. For if the farm were sold, *she* would be sold, and so would her children, and goodness knows where they would all finish up, and she might never see Sam, her husband, again. Something must be done quickly.

Myfanwy stood quietly in the sty with the piglets dashing round her, and had a good think. If she could teach the children to rootle and clear the land, perhaps that would bring in a bit of money. But they very seldom got out. So Myfanwy tried to see if she could open the door of the sty. To her great delight, this proved quite easy as the wood was rotten with the damp, and the hinges were coming away. One bang with her snout and it would be down. Perhaps Gwilym Ifan and Maggie would both go out one day together and then she would have her chance.

And I am glad to say that during the very next week they had an invitation to spend a day at the sea, and Myfanwy waited until she saw them safely down the road before she hit the gate hard with her head and down it fell. She trotted, grunting, into the yard with the piglets following delightedly. But Ginger played a silly waiting-behind-game, so that Myfanwy had to go back to look for him, when he rushed squealing past her. Then she took them all down the muddy track to the wilderness of scrub and thorn, and gave them their first rootling lesson. They soon began to enjoy themselves.

'No, no, like this, Ginger,' said Myfanwy, sticking her large black behind right across the track. And at that moment some hikers were passing, and one of them tapped Myfanwy politely on the rump and said, 'The pig track is a good path up Snowdon.' And the other hiker said, 'I wonder why it is called the Pig Track?'

And the first hiker said, 'Perhaps it is a special place for pigs. Let's go and see.'

A SPECIAL PLACE FOR PIGS!!! The pig track . . . Myfanwy stopped rootling and thought quickly. Something in her long-way-back-pig-fairyblood stirred . . . and she knew, as certainly as the rooster crows at dawn, that she must follow these hikers and find out.

She gave a tremendous squeal to round up the family and set off after the hikers. She kept fairly far away so as not to arouse their suspicions, and soon found that they were making towards Snowdon. They climbed and climbed and eventually stopped at the hotel at the top of Llanberis Pass. Myfanwy tried to keep the family behind a stone wall, because someone would be bound to start a hullaballoo if they saw a large black sow and five piglets running about on the main road to Caernarfon.

Presently the hikers came out and started off up the

mountain. Myfanwy scampered out from behind the wall, followed by Blodwen, Ceinwen, Josephine and Dimple, but Ginger was again giving trouble and trying to be funny. His mother cuffed him with her snout and he squealed. Myfanwy rushed on ahead, hoping that no one would hear them in the hotel or the cottages by the road, and she got nearer to the hikers than she had meant.

However, they were talking and did not hear her grunts. Soon the track got very steep indeed, and one of the hikers turned round. 'Look at that,' he cried. 'Pigs!'

'Pigs on the pig track,' said the other hiker. 'How wonderful.'

And as they didn't seem to mind Myfanwy and the children, she went scampering on, for she felt that somewhere up in the dark recesses of the mountain was a place where she could get help for the farm and her family.

Then Ginger squealed and stood still, and Myfanwy, good mother that she was, realised that the family had had enough, and that it was time they went. But she looked up to the towering crags above her, and knew as certainly as there was water in Llyn Gwynant that she would have to come back, and alone. Then she called the family and started off home. It was much later than she supposed, and twice she lost Ginger, who was really getting very spoiled and naughty. In fact, it was almost dark when they reached the farm gate. Then what Myfanwy most feared would happen had happened. Gwilym-Ifan and Maggie had got home first, and found the gate down and the pigsty empty.

That meant a new gate and the end of her hopes of salvation. She trotted sadly back into the yard, followed by the tired piglets. Gwilym-Ifan was so pleased to see her that he never scolded her, but just shut her up, gave her some food, and said goodnight, adding, 'To-morrow we must mend the gate, cariad bach; we do not want to lose you. For when we sell the farm, we are going to buy a nice bungalow at Porthmadog, and the missus says when she sells you she is going to buy some nice new furniture on the H.P. But, indeed, cariad bach, I do not want to part with you,' he finished sentimentally. And then he started to sing a sad Welsh air, and Myfanwy forgave him everything: his bad noisy ways, his drinking at the Goat, his spend-thriftness and all his other sins.

Tomorrow came and tomorrow Gwilym-Ifan did nothing about the gate; in fact, it was nearly always tomorrow with him, but, alas! Maggie passed the sty and said, 'Gwilym-Ifan, aren't you going to mend the pigsty? We do not want to lose the old sow again!'

And just as poor Myfanwy was wondering what piece of furniture she would be exchanged for, Gwilym Ifan came with the end of an old iron bedstead and wired it round the post. Poor Myfanwy sank down in despair. For now she knew only too well that she MUST get out, that she must go up that mountain, for there alone could she save the farm and the family.

She went to bed that night and cried herself to sleep, a thing she had not done since she was a piglet. And then she had a most wonderful dream, for she dreamt that she saw her fairy ancestor sitting on a cloud wearing a crown of stars and a daisy chain, and her fairy ancestor said, 'Myfanwy, you have been a good sow, and we want to do all we can to help you. Go out in the morning and push the post that the bedstead is tied to, and you will find it is as rotten as the gate, and I will meet you on Snowdon.' And then she woke up and heard the roosters crowing in the valley. And she trotted out quietly and pushed the post, and sure enough, it was rotten, and nearly fell over there and then. And it would have been just the wrong moment for Maggie was coming out into the yard to feed the hens.

It would have to be at night, and soon, as the piglets were getting big, and Myfanwy was terribly afraid. All next week it was cold and stormy, with snow on the mountain, and then at last on the Saturday it cleared, and the clouds rolled away, and Glyder Fach shone in the evening light, and a large full moon came up in the sky like a yellow cheese. Myfanwy put the children to bed and hoped they would sleep; then she waited for Gwilym-Ifan to come in, for she knew he would be late, as it was Saturday. And late he was indeed, for the moon was high in the sky and the valley bright with its light by the time he banged the cottage door. Myfanwy waited until she saw the candles go upstairs, and the quarrelling start in the bedroom, and then she gave the post a hard push. She prayed that the bedstead would fall quietly, which, indeed, it did, but loud enough for Gwilym-Ifan to open the window and shout, 'Who is there?'

Myfanwy stood like a black shadow until he shut the window again. Then she trotted silently down on to the road. After that she galloped, praying that there would be no cars, and she got nearly as far as Pen-y Gwryd when she saw one coming. Myfanwy pretended to be a big milestone, and shut her eyes tight so that they would not catch the lights of the car as it passed. Then she rushed up the road to the pass. Just as she turned up the pig track, she saw two late cyclists. One of them said, 'Look, a pig.' And the other screamed and swore that Myfanwy was a ghost.

She ran on and on and up and up, into the moonlight, and it got colder and colder and higher and higher, and suddenly a white mist shadowed the moon, and Myfanwy heard music. And soon the path crossed a small stream and she drank thirstily. She saw before her a sheet of clear dark water surrounded by black cliffs, and from over the other side of the lake came the sound of voices. Pig voices, all singing something wonderful that Myfanwy had heard while scratching her back near the wireless in the farm kitchen. Yes, it was the 'Hallelujah' Chorus from Handel's *Messiah*. As it seemed a terribly long way round the lake, Myfanwy plunged in, and swam across and, though she was very tired, she emerged much fresher and ran up the slope towards the music. Then she stopped and stood in amazement, for there before her in a hollow of the mountain was a great circular arena, and in it were pigs and pigs and pigs. And they were all singing, and it was the most wonderful singing that Myfanwy had ever heard. There were pigs as far as the eye could see, all singing away gloriously in a light that seemed stronger than the moonlight. And then a great voice cried, 'Myfanwy, Myfanwy from Coed Uchaf Farm; come down here.' And though Myfanwy was a little bit frightened, she trotted down the steps of the arena past the rows of singing pigs. And in the middle of the arena stood her fairy grandmother, who kissed her, while Myfanwy asked who all the other pigs were.

'They are pigs who have died,' was the reply. 'And they come here twice a year to sing. We know that you are in trouble, so we are giving you this key. Go straight home and take the children out rootling; but whatever happens, do not lose the key. Now goodbye, and God speed, for you must be home before dawn.'

So Myfanwy did not ask any more questions, but trotted back up the steps. And some of the pigs looked at her over their music, but did not stop singing. And presently she reached the top of the amphitheatre and looked down. The pigs were singing softly now, and Myfanwy shut her eyes and thanked God for the beauty of the sound.

Reluctantly she turned her back on the pig choirs and scampered down the side of the mountain and swam across the lake with the golden key in her mouth. She dashed past the quarrymen's cottages as there were lights in some of the upper windows, and she feared some of the poor quarrymen might think she would make a good Sunday dinner. Then she found the short cut home and ran on and on until she came to the farm. Then, tired and worn out as she was, she woke the children and drove them out rootling. And they started to rootle and rootle and rootle, and the moonlight faded and the dawn came. The cocks crew and far away the dogs barked and still they rootled and poor, tired Myfanwy stood patiently by with the golden key in her mouth. And then suddenly Dimple gave a squeal and called Josephine, and Josephine gave a squeal and fetched Blodwen, who fetched Ceinwen, who tried to fetch Ginger, who was doing something silly by a fence. And they all stood round one spot and rootled and squealed until their poor mother just had to see what it was all about. And

31

here, to her amazement, partly concealed in the earth, lay a huge wooden box. It was too heavy for them to get out, so Myfanwy sent the pigs home one by one to fetch Gwilym-Ifan. And at last she could stay awake no longer and lay down and slept on the ground beside the wooden box with the key in her mouth. And that was how Gwilym-Ifan found her, and he took the key and opened the box, which was found to contain pieces and pieces of gold and jewels and other treasures.

And so Myfanwy saved the farm and her family, for Gwilym kept all the girls and married them to husbands in Capel Curig, and they all rootled and rootled and rootled and cleared all his land, and he planted grass and potatoes and trees, and became richer and happier and far more reliable.

Ginger he kept for a pet and Myfanwy for luck. And they lived happily ever afterwards. Much later, when her time came, Myfanwy joined the pig choir and became one of the leading sopranos.

CYRIL THE SEED (or THE PEACEFUL BEAN)

Cyril, the seed, lay cold and dry and still in a packet of beans marked, 'Dwarf Canadian Wonder' in the ironmonger's shop in Welshpool.

He slept just like the other beans, but he did not look like them, and how he came to be in that packet nobody knows.

One frosty February afternoon, little Mr. Jones, Post Office, Llanfair—up in the hills—came and bought the packet, and Cyril fell down sleepily among the others.

'Bit early for beans, isn't it, Mr. Jones?' said Mr. Preece, the assistant with the crinkly hair.

'Well, yes, indeed,' said Mr. Jones. 'But I have got a little greenhouse at the back with a bit of heat, and I want to try and force them along. I've got some nice big pots I used last year for the tomatoes.'

'Oh, yes indeed, very good idea,' said Mr. Preece, thinking now about his sweetheart. 'Can I put them in a bag for you?'

'No, thank you,' said Mr. Jones. 'I'll put them in the pocket of my old mac,' and he laughed and rubbed his glasses with a silk handkerchief, because he was very short-sighted indeed.

Then he put the beans in his pocket and climbed into his dog cart and called up his old grey mare, Lady, and drove off through the frosty evening up the grey winding road to his village in the hills. His wife was waiting for him with the lamps lit and a lovely tea, and he told her all that he had done during the day, and took the packet of beans out of his pocket.

'I'm going to try these in the greenhouse,' he said. 'With that bit of heat they ought to come along nicely.'

'Beans in February,' said his wife kindly. 'What will you think of next?'

And then as the shop bell tinkled, Mrs. Jones went into the Post Office and Mr. Jones put the packet of beans on the window sill among the geraniums and turned on the wireless to see if there was going to be a change in the weather.

And next day he went out into his little greenhouse

and prepared and sifted the soil, the compost, the sand and the lime, and filled the large tomato pots. Then he took the seeds out of the packet, where Cyril was lying near the top, and Mr. Jones picked them up lovingly and buried them in the soil, about six to each pot.

Now had he not been so short-sighted, he would have noticed something very strange indeed about Cyril; for he was not purple at all, but bright yellow with red spots. He was gay and happy-looking, like something out of a circus. But he went into the pot just the same, down into the beautiful damp earth that Mr. Jones had prepared.

Then Mr. Jones shut up the windows tight against the frost, stoked his little boiler, whistled a happy tune and went to help his wife in the shop.

Mrs. Jones was bustling about, serving soap, cheese and bacon, when in came some Italian farm labourers that worked at Cefn-y-Maes Farm. They had not been in Britain very long, and could speak neither English nor Welsh. Mr. Jones was standing staring and thinking about his beans, and Mrs. Jones got rather cross and said:

'Try to make them understand. I can't make out a word they say.'

But Mr. Jones was no better at Italian than his wife, and in the end the Italians had to draw a picture of a mousetrap, which is what they wanted.

And the days grew longer and lighter, and every

day Mr. Jones went into his greenhouse to look at his pots. But as yet there was nothing stirring in the soil.

Now Mr. Jones had a small friend, a boy called Johnny Lewis, who was as fond of gardening as he was. He used to run in every day to see the greenhouse on his way to school.

'How are the beans coming along, Mr. Jones?' he would shout if he was late. 'Anything showing yet?'

'Early days, my boy,' Mr. Jones would reply. 'We must be patient in the garden.'

'If I were you,' Johnny shouted back, 'I would dig one up and see if they're starting. I once had a broad bean in school in a jar and I watched it growing every day through the glass.'

And Mr. Jones clucked like a broody hen and pretended to be shocked, but he, too, had really longed to look down into the dark earth in his pots and see what was going on. And if they had been made of glass he would have seen that the beans were stirring to life, that they were pushing up through the soil with their heads bent reverently down, like people in chapel.

Then one wonderful Saturday morning there was one showing, and by the afternoon there were three, and by Sunday morning, just as Mr. Jones was getting ready for chapel, there were five, and one of the five was Cyril.

Mr. Jones rushed in and called his wife, and said:

'Martha, cariad, there are five of my beans up in the greenhouse.'

And Mrs. Jones called back, 'You and your old beans; we shall be late for chapel with that new preacher coming from Llan Rhaiadr and me in my new hat. Come on, Mr. Jones bach, come on.'

And Mr. Jones hid his delight and followed her to chapel, watching the darkening sky, and hoping that it was not snow.

Mr. Pugh, the new preacher, preached a very long, very wonderful sermon about the Tower of Babel, and Mrs. Jones cried with the other ladies; but I am sorry to say that Mr. Jones was watching the snowstorm and thinking about his beans. After chapel he almost ran home with Johnny Lewis running behind and shouting, 'Can I come and see the beans, Mr. Jones?'

Together they went into the little greenhouse where it was warm, 60° by the thermometer, and stood and looked at the beans.

'Look,' said Johnny, 'that one looks like a man standing with his arms stretched out.'

And they looked at all the seeds lovingly, while the spring snow fell softly on the greenhouse roof and melted away.

Cyril was there, too, with his head bowed and his arms folded, and he looked no different from the other beans; though we shall soon learn how different he was.

Next day Mr. Jones had to go to Shrewsbury to get some new glasses, and when he came back, the strangest thing had occurred. For there in the pot with the ordinary french bean seedlings was a plant with bright yellow leaves spotted with red. And that plant was Cyril.

Mr. Jones cried out in horror, because now that he was wearing his new glasses he could see only too clearly Cyril's curious colour. He was as surprised as the other beans had been when Cyril opened up, and his first thought was to root him up and throw him away, thinking that he had some awful blight.

But Cyril was saved by Johnny, who came running into the greenhouse. 'Look at that wonderful bean!' he cried. 'It looks like a leopard!'

'Wonderful, is it?' said Mr. Jones, doubtfully. 'I was thinking that it was maybe a disease and that I probably ought to throw it away so that the others wouldn't catch it.'

'Oh no, no,' cried Johnny. 'I am sure it is special, it is magic, it is something wonderful!' and as he said this, the greenhouse door banged to, and Mr. Jones scratched his head and wondered how such a thing could happen on a still day.

And so Cyril's life was saved, and he grew up like the other beans and flowered, and his flowers were a beautiful rose colour, and when his pods came, they were spotted with red. Mrs. Jones, who was longing for an early dish of beans, had decided that Cyril must be poisonous, and that though he was very pretty, he must not be eaten. Then, when the other beans were ready, she asked Johnny Lewis and his mother to dinner and sent Mr. Jones out to the greenhouse to pick the beans, telling him on no account to pick Cyril.

So Mr. Jones took off his glasses to clean them, put them down on the shelf in the greenhouse, and tried to find his handkerchief. When he had found it, his glasses seemed somehow to have disappeared, and so he fumbled round the bean plants and picked all the beans that were ready.

And Cyril knew that his hour had come, and as soon as he was picked, he turned himself into an ordinary french bean so that when Mrs. Jones came to top and tail him she did not guess that she was topping and tailing a magic bean.

Just as Mrs Jones was putting the beans on to cook, Johnny Lewis ran in as usual and said breathlessly:

'Oh, Mrs. Jones, Mam is so sorry but she says can she bring the little Italian girl, Anna Maria, as she cannot leave her all alone, as her parents have gone to Welshpool.'

Mrs. Jones tried not to look annoyed, and said, 'That's all right, Johnny, except that no one will be able to understand a word she says,' and went on laying the table.

And then Mrs. Lewis arrived with little Anna Maria, dark-eyed and serious, and they all sat down to a wonderful dinner of roast lamb, roast potatoes and French beans. Mr. Jones was very proud and helped everybody to the beans himself. And somehow Cyril managed to get himself on to every plate. Before they ate the beans, Mr. Jones said, 'First beans of the year: we must all wish.'

And as Anna Maria swallowed the first mouthful, she said, 'I wish I could learn to speak English!'

Mr. Jones put down his fork with a clatter. 'What was that you said?'

And the little girl said again, 'I wish that I could learn to speak English.'

'Who taught you to say that?' Mr. Jones asked.

And Anna Maria replied, 'Nobody; I can just speak, that is all.'

And she turned to Mr. Jones and spoke in Italian, and Mr. Jones swallowed a mouthful and found himself answering. And before they knew where they were, they were all jabbering away in Italian. Nobody seemed to find it in the least strange, and, indeed, everyone was very happy, and the party was a great success. Anna Maria went home a much less sad and serious little person than she had been before.

While Mrs. Jones was washing the dishes, Mr. Jones went into the greenhouse, and there amongst the seed boxes he found his glasses. He cleaned them with

40

his silk handkerchief and then looked round at the
beans. To his horror he saw that he had picked all the
beans off Cyril and realised that they must have all
eaten them. He scratched his head and did not know
what to do. It was now some time after dinner; in fact,
Mr. Jones was beginning to feel like a cup of tea. He
certainly did not feel any ill effects. But what about
his wife and friends who had come to dinner?

And then suddenly he remembered. The gift of
tongues! Of course! There was something about it in
the Bible. They had all eaten a dish of beans and they
had all understood one another. They had all been
friends.

He rushed into the house to ask his wife if she
remembered how they had all spoken different
languages after that dish of beans. Mr. Jones was very
excited, but his wife looked at him awkwardly. She
was a sensible woman, and did not welcome fancy
ideas.

'Yes, I do remember you jabbering away like an
Italian,' she said.

'And you did too, cariad,' said Mr. Jones. 'It must
have been the beans.'

'Beans?' said Mrs. Jones. 'What beans?'

'Why, the red and yellow spotted ones . . .' But he
had said too much. Mrs. Jones was pale and horrified.

'Those terrible poisonous things; do you mean you
picked those?'

'Why, yes dear,' said Mr. Jones. 'I am afraid I took the wrong beans because I lost my glasses '

'Then we shall all die in the night,' said Mrs. Jones dramatically, and made a pot of tea.

I am afraid Mr. Jones was in disgrace that night and for a few days afterwards. All next week they ate French beans, but he made sure not to pick Cyril. However, he realised that very soon the beans would be over and that he would need the pots for his tomatoes. There stood Cyril covered in pods, waiting to be picked and dried. Should he save the seed of what he felt was a magic bean? He was too afraid of what his wife would say if she saw him growing the bean again. So he picked six or seven pods absentmindedly and put them in his pocket, and decided that it would be better to throw the plant away. It was then that Johnny came running into the greenhouse.

'Surely you are not going to throw away those lovely pods?' he said, gazing lovingly at Cyril.

'Well, indeed,' said Mr. Jones. 'My wife thinks they are the invention of the devil, and I am afraid she will be very cross if they come up again.'

'I don't think that they're anything of the kind. I think they are lovely. Please, Mr. Jones, may I keep some?'

And so Mr. Jones picked some speckled pods and gave them to Johnny. And Johnny put them in his pocket and went home happily. But, alas! he did not know that he had a hole in his pocket, and that by the time he got home, all the seeds had gone.

Meanwhile, as Mr. Jones sifted the soil for his tomato plants he could not bring himself to throw Cyril away.

One warm evening in April, Mr. Jones and Johnny Lewis set out together for a walk that they always took once a year. Up to the top of a hill crowned with a little tump of cedar trees, to look for a green linnet's nest and to see a wild cherry tree in flower.

There was a wonderful view from the top of the old tump, all over towards the Wrekin and the plain stretching away to the Potteries and back to the hills of Wales crowding away to the west.

The tump, it is said, was an old burial ground after a battle. It was also said that here Owain Glyndŵr had fought the English. Johnny's head was full of dreams of clashing swords and knights in armour and beautiful maidens; while poor Mr. Jones was thinking about a pot in his greenhouse containing a strange spotted bean that had the gift of tongues.

It was such a lovely evening they stayed longer than they should have done, until the weltering sun made long shadows on the grass of the tump, and a small wind stirred the topmost boughs of the cedars.

Suddenly, up the old track that ran through the

bracken, they saw a man on horseback. Both he and
the horse looked tired, and they walked slowly to the
top of the hill, and the man dismounted and looked
across the distant plain. Then he spoke to the horse:

'We have failed, my friend,' he said. 'This lovely
land should have been one kingdom, but it never will
be. The peoples of the earth should be as one person,
but they never will be. Not so long as one nation
speaks a language that the other does not understand. I
was a peaceful man in my green acres, but I had to go
to war for my people. And where are my warriors
now? Dead . . . scattered across the plains of Powys
and the vales of Ceiriog and Edyrnion. Hiding in the
mountain retreats of Gwynedd.'

And as he spoke, he turned and looked fully at
Johnny and Mr. Jones, and the last oblique golden
rays of the setting sun caught his face in a halo of
light and shone in his wonderful tired eyes.

And Johnny gasped in ecstasy, and Mr. Jones
looked down and rubbed his glasses.

'Dear friends,' said the man. 'If this beautiful world
is to survive the evil passions of mankind, we must
learn to understand one another, to speak to each
other. I have lost the cause of my people, but my
longbowmen will go to fight against another people
speaking another language. And so it will go on until
the peoples of the earth can speak to each other
without fear. . . .'

Then he turned and mounted his horse, and turned its head towards the south.

'God speed you, my friends,' the tired man said sadly. 'I must find shelter in the borderlands, away from my beloved country.'

And as he rode away, Johnny clutched Mr. Jones by the arm and burst out: 'Did you see his armour under his cloak? He was a great hero! It must have been . . .'

'I saw no armour,' said Mr. Jones, 'only a tired man speaking the truth. But then, I cannot see much without my spectacles. Come, Johnny bach, it is very late: we must go home.'

And though he and Johnny never mentioned a word to each other about the stranger, Mr. Jones was thinking furiously all the way home. What the man had said was true. If the peoples of the world could understand one another, there would be no wars. And he, Morgan Dafydd Jones, son of Evan Jones, Hendre Bach, had in his greenhouse a spotted bean with the gift of tongues that could save all mankind.

He *must* therefore save the seed of the bean, no matter what his wife said, and grow it again next year, and take it up to London and get all the ladies and gentlemen who ruled the world to eat the beans so that they might speak each other's language.

And when he got back home, though he was very late, Mrs. Jones did not scold him—only gave him a lovely tea with home-made currant cakes and jam and bread and butter and a boiled egg.

'I've got a surprise for you,' she said. 'While you were out, I thought I would do a bit of tidying up for you in your greenhouse. Your tomatoes are looking champion, and I burnt that nasty old bean in the corner.'

'You what?' said Mr. Jones in terror.

'I burnt that old bean,' she said.

'Oh! Martha, cariad, what did you do that for?' said poor Mr. Jones, almost in tears.

'Well, it was dead, wasn't it?' she replied, 'and untidy.'

Mr. Jones could say no more. He just drank his tea sadly, his glasses misting over so that he could hardly see the currants in the cake.

After tea he went out with a torch to the greenhouse and looked at the empty pot where Cyril had been, and it may have been his imagination, but he thought it glowed with a strange light.

And he went to bed with a heavy heart.

Next February he sifted the soil and planted the beans as before, but he did not feel at all excited about them, and so he did not notice that he put his hand in his pocket for his handkerchief and shook out some of Cyril's seeds that were left from last year.

(But Cyril knew that his children were safely in the soil, and he was determined that this year he and Mr. Jones should succeed.)

On the wireless and in the newspapers there were wars and rumours of wars, and they went as far as to pray for peace in the chapel one Sunday morning. After chapel Mr. Jones went into his greenhouse and there were his beans, too, praying with their heads bent in the soil. Mr. Jones took off his spectacles and said, 'If only these beans had been any spotted ones, I could have done something with them to help the cause of peace,' and as he spoke there was a strange buzzing sound, and there, standing in one of the pots with his arms outstretched, was one of Cyril's children, a yellow and red spotted bean!

Next day there were more and more. And Mr. Jones, his heart full of joy, prayed in a loud voice: 'Oh, Lord, I am a good and loving husband, but please keep my wife out of the greenhouse until my peaceful spotted beans shall be ready to eat.'

And the Lord heard Mr. Jones' prayer and sent Mrs. Jones for four weeks holiday to her sister in Aberystwyth.

While she was away, the beans flowered and the pods grew, and when she came back, Mr. Jones determined to be brave and tell her what he planned to do. He went to the station to meet her, and as Mrs. Jones bustled out of the train, laden with parcels, he blurted out, 'Martha, I have been deceiving you.'

Mrs. Jones dropped her parcels, but before she had time to answer, he continued:

'The greenhouse is full of speckled beans, and they are not the invention of the devil, and I am going up to London with them to give them to the ladies and gentlemen who rule the world, so that they will understand one another.'

'Cariad, bach,' said Mrs. Jones, kindly, 'I shall never go to Aberystwyth again if this is how it takes you,' and she bustled him into the little post office and stoked up the fire and made him a lovely tea with some fancy icing cakes she had bought for him in Aberystwyth. But though Mr. Jones loved icing cakes, he went on talking:

'Martha, you must listen to me, you must help me,' he pleaded. 'This is my task, the great good deed I can do to help the world.'

'How can I help you?' she said, 'when we know no one in London, and anyway, no one would eat those awful beans if they saw them growing.'

So they spoke no more of Cyril, but unpacked and had a look at Mrs. Jones' new costume and hat, and then they listened to the news and went to bed.

In a few days' time Mr. Jones bravely picked his beans and put them in a paper bag, packed a small case and went and told his wife that he was going to London.

Mrs. Jones, being a sensible woman, and seeing the look in her husband's eye, said nothing.

So Mr. Jones harnessed his grey mare, Lady, and

left her at the station with little Johnny. He got into the train, and wondered how he was going to accomplish this great task—he, a little short-sighted postmaster with a bag of speckled beans, from a village on the Welsh border. He would have to trust in God and the power of his magic bean.

The local train stopped at most of the stations before getting to Shrewsbury, but usually only if there was someone waiting. And when it stopped at Old Tump Station, a man got into the carriage carrying a very large book. Mr. Jones said, 'Good morning,' politely, and when the stranger looked up Mr. Jones seemed to remember something about his face.

'Are you going to London?' asked the stranger.

'Yes,' said Mr. Jones, hoping that he would not ask which part of London.

'Do you know many people in London, may I ask?'

'No,' said Mr. Jones, humbly. 'I don't know anybody.'

'Are you going on holiday, then?' asked the stranger kindly.

'Why, no,' said Mr. Jones awkwardly, furiously cleaning his glasses. 'I am going to try and help somebody.' He didn't know what else to say.

Then the stranger took a letter out of the large book he was carrying. 'Take this letter and go to the address on it, and give it to the person to whom it is addressed. This person will be able to help you, I know.'

The stranger stood up, and there was something so commanding about his voice that Mr. Jones took the envelope meekly.

As the stranger was opening the door of the carriage, he turned and wished Mr. Jones Godspeed. And Mr. Jones put on his glasses and looked into his eyes, and they were the eyes of the tired man who had ridden up to him and Johnny in the bracken, the tired man who spoke the truth.

When Mr. Jones got out of the little train to change on to the express, he asked the guard, 'Who was the gentleman who got into my carriage at Old Tump Halt?'

The guard looked puzzled, and said, 'I think you must be mistaken, sir; we didn't stop at Old Tump Halt: we haven't done for six years.'

Mr. Jones got into the London train with a strange, dry, excited feeling in his throat.

When he got to London he took a taxi to the address on the envelope that the stranger had given him. It was a small side street off a busy road, and the taxi stopped outside a dairy. Mr. Jones was very relieved indeed to find that they were Welsh people called Ellis, from Trawsfynydd. A jolly girl serving the milk and eggs took Mr. Jones to the back kitchen and gave the letter to her brother, to whom it was addressed.

He looked at Mr. Jones and said, 'I believe you have a parcel for me?'

'Why, yes,' said Mr. Jones, opening his case and producing his paper bag. 'My beans, Mr. Ellis. I grew them, but do not be astonished at their strange colour.'

'Never fear, Mr. Jones,' said the young man. 'I have been expecting you.'

And Mr. Jones timidly opened the paper bag, and shook the beans out onto the table. To his horror, they looked just like ordinary beans! Surely he could not have been so stupid as that? Surely he had not picked the wrong ones?

'Oh, dear,' said Mr. Jones. 'I hope they are all right. They seem to have changed colour.'

And Mr. Ellis said, 'Let's see,' and bit into a bean. Immediately he started talking French.

Neither Mr. Jones nor young David Ellis knew that Cyril had taught his children to look as like ordinary beans as he had done the first day that he was topped and tailed by Mrs. Jones.

Young Mr. Ellis went off to work in the evening, taking with him the paper bag containing Cyril's children. Mr. Jones was invited to stay at the dairy, and as he had never been to London before, Miss Ellis took him for a walk to show him the lights.

Later in the evening they sat and listened to the wireless. And on the news it said that the heads of two great nations were dining together, and that the fate of these countries depended upon what happened at the banquet.

Mr. Jones looked at Miss Ellis, and Miss Ellis said, 'Yes, you are quite right. My brother is a cook, the assistant to the head chef.' And before Mr. Jones could say anything else, some choirs came on, and he forgot all about his beans in the glory of their singing.

The next morning he caught the 9.10 train back to Shrewsbury, and in the papers he read that the great powers had parted on the most friendly terms and that they had spoken together freely. Mr. Jones said a small prayer of thanksgiving as the train passed through Princes Risborough station. He knew now that his journey had not been in vain.

His wife met him at the station and they went home to their little white Post Office and had tea in front of the fire. Mr. Jones went out afterwards to look at his beans. Everything seemed very orderly in the greenhouse, but nowhere could he see a speckled bean. Only the ordinary dwarf Canadian Wonder.

'Perhaps, after all, it was a disease,' thought Mr. Jones.

Later in the year he took his wife to London, and they tried to find the dairy, but though he found the street and the other shops, in the place where the dairy should have been there stood a shop selling foreign books.

Mr. Jones decided that it must be because he had his wrong glasses. So he took Mrs. Jones round the shops and they caught the 4.10 back to Shrewsbury and went happily home to their little Post Office in Llanfair on the road to the mountains. And, indeed, they liked Llanfair much better than London.

They both lived happily for a long while, but though Mr. Jones was always looking, never again did he see a speckled bean like Cyril.

THE PEPPER POT OFFICE

Little Mr. Jenkins worked in a large red brick building in Cardiff. It was one of those middle-aged buildings that had survived the bombing, and had been built in the reign of Queen Victoria. It had windows like a church, high draughty offices, and at each corner a small overhanging room with windows on three sides, which looked like a pepper pot.

Every Day, Mr. Jenkins added up rows and rows of tiny figures which had made him very short-sighted. He was known to the other people in the building as 'Jenkins bach', as there was another, taller and younger Mr. Jenkins.

At the top of the red brick building was a very large room lit from the top by light coming through a grand and gloomy glass dome. The glass was stained the colour of weak tea, and made everybody in the room look very pasty, as though they needed a holiday, which indeed, most of them did.

And in this room lived and worked Mr. Oliver Cromwell Jones.

Now everybody was terrified of Mr. Oliver Cromwell Jones. He was the boss, and though he was nearly always sitting under the weak tea-coloured glass, he seemed to be everywhere, and to see and hear and know everything.

But there was one thing that he did not know, or had not yet found out, and that was that when little Mr. Jenkins had applied for the job in the red brick building, he had made himself out to be eight years younger than he actually was.

And that was why Mr. Jenkins was more frightened of Mr. Oliver Cromwell Jones than anyone else.

Mr. Jenkins lived in a street in Canton, off the Cowbridge road. It bore the name of a country district where there were mountains and trees and rivers and quiet places, where one could hear nothing but the voices of the larks and curlews, and where there was no Mr. Oliver Cromwell Jones.

And though Mr. Jenkins loved the city and the docks and the kind and cheerful people, he sometimes longed almost unbearably to go back to the village in the Monmouthshire valley, on the way to the Black Mountains, where he had been born sixty one years ago.

But there was no chance of that.

Upstairs in the front bedroom of the house in the terrace in Canton, lay his grand-daughter Dilys, unable to do anything but lie there and watch the television. Her parents were both dead, and though Mr. Jenkins had tried everything that the National Health would provide, she never seemed to get any stronger, except when he took her on his fortnight's holiday to the Mumbles or the Gower coast, when she seemed to get better every minute, and to be able to sit up in her chair on the beach. If only he could make a lot of money and get her away to the country, he knew that she would be all right and grow up strong and healthy like other children.

But what chance was there of making a fortune in the red brick building? Year in, year out, life seemed to go on the same dreary way.

Until one particular hot and stifling afternoon in July, when Mr. Jenkins was longing for his holiday, and the buzzer which showed that Mr. Oliver Cromwell Jones was going to speak started. Then someone upstairs switched on, and a dry and rasping voice asked would Mr. Isaac Jenkins please go upstairs at once to Mr. Oliver Cromwell Jones's office.

The other boys working with Mr. Jenkins patted him on the back and wished him luck, saying how glad they were that it wasn't them. Then Mr. Jenkins, his heart in his boots, went into the passage, stepped into the wobbly old lift and pulled himself up by the rope.

The lift opened immediately into Mr. Oliver Cromwell Jones's office so that there was no time even to clear one's throat or straighten one's tie before facing him.

Mr. Oliver Cromwell Jones glared at him as he shut the lift gate.

'Ah yes, Mr. Jenkins,' he said in his high harsh voice, 'won't you sit down a minute?'

Mr. Jenkins trembled for Mr. Oliver Cromwell Jones never asked anyone to sit down unless something dreadful had happened.

'A little matter of figures,' he said, and hunched his shoulders and settled his face with its high beaklike nose into his neck, just like a buzzard that Mr. Jenkins had seen sitting on a rock when he went for a holiday in north Wales.

What, thought poor little Mr. Jenkins, have I done wrong now?

'I have a very ticklish job here' said Mr. Oliver Cromwell Jones, not coming to the point at once, in order to keep Mr. Jenkins guessing. 'And I thought you might be able to help me.'

'Why, yes of course,' said Mr. Jenkins, 'anything I can do . . .'

'It isn't just anything' said Mr. Oliver Cromwell Jones severely. 'It's the Whitland case, very ticklish indeed; this man must owe the State a lot of money and it is our duty to find out how much. I thought you might be the person for the job. All the papers are in the little office at the corner of the building. Here are the keys. There are all sorts of secret documents and I want a full report drawn up. Of course, you will get overtime for doing this.'

Mr. Jenkins' heart sang. Overtime, money, more money! That meant that he would be able to put a few more pounds under his mattress and perhaps make the down payment at last on the cottage and the acre of land in the Vale of Glamorgan that he wanted so badly for himself and Dilys.

'Thank you, thank you,' he muttered, going over towards Mr. Oliver Cromwell Jones, who stood over him like a great black bird.

'Not at all, my dear fellow. With your record and your experience, you were the obvious choice.' Mr. Oliver Cromwell Jones settled back into his chair under the stained glass.

Mr. Jenkins went towards the lift, gratefully clinking the keys.

'I should start right away if I were you,' said Mr. Oliver Cromwell Jones, 'no time to be lost.'

And as Mr. Jenkins opened the gates he added, 'By the way, Mrs. Oliver Cromwell Jones and I took a run through your home county last night. Very pretty indeed, your Monmouthshire. We stopped and looked at the church in your native village, no doubt you were baptised there. Very pleasant indeed.'

And Mr. Jenkins's heart sank with the lift.

So that was it.

Mr. Oliver Cromwell Jones had been snooping again. Who knows if he had not already looked in the parish register and found out that he, Isaac Thomas Jenkins, was really sixty-one instead of fifty-three.

He went miserably back into his office.

The other boys wanted to know what had happened and could not understand why he seemed so sad.

And when Mr. Jenkins went into the little pepper pot office, he didn't know why he was sad either.

Because everything in there was delightful. To begin with, there was the view over and about the city, and as the little pepper pot overhung the street it was almost like being in an aeroplane, though Mr. Jenkins, of course, had never been able to afford that.

The walls of the office were covered with pictures of castles and mansions and great Spanish galleons and the chair was on a swivel and unbelievably comfortable.

Mr. Jenkins could not believe his luck. Just wait until he got home to tell Dilys.

And the time flew by until they were ready to go for their August holiday, and Mr. Jenkins locked up the pepperpot office and gave the key to Mr. Oliver Cromwell Jones's secretary. Then he packed himself and Dilys off to Oxwich Bay on the Gower Peninsula, where they sat all day on the sands and went back to a kind landlady in the evening.

And one night Mr. Jenkins had a funny dream: he dreamt that he was walking round the red brick building and looking at the pepper pot office. All round the building he walked, and to his great surprise he found that there were not as he supposed, four pepperpots, one at each corner, but only three. This did not worry him unduly, except that he made sure that when he went back to Cardiff, he would walk round the building to see that they were all there.

And this year instead of dreading the return to work, he rather looked forward to it.

And the first morning when he got to the red brick building the doorman told him how well he was looking, and he ran upstairs without waiting for the lift, so anxious was he to get back to his pepperpot office.

He ran along the passage and opened the door. Everything in the cosy little room seemed the same. Only one thing puzzled him, and that was the work. Somehow he did not remember having got on so quickly, did not remember having done so much.

Anyway, whatever had happened was for the best, and he soon handed in his first report to Mr. Oliver Cromwell Jones.

And soon also he had a nice wad of overtime pound notes which he put with his other meagre savings under the mattress. Then one day at the end of September, a curious thing happened. He met a friend on the bus going to work, a friend who had once worked in the red brick building but had now retired. Mr. Jenkins was very pleased to see him and tell him about his new job.

'That's funny,' said his friend, 'I once got shifted into that little office at the end of the building, and it brought me luck too.'

'Lovely view, isn't it?' said Mr. Jenkins, 'right over towards the mountains and the valleys.'

'No,' said his friend, 'you couldn't see the valleys from that office; the little office on the valleys side is just there for show. There is no floor or anything like that, it is just to make the building look even all round. There are only three real offices.'

And Mr. Jenkins would like to have argued about that, but as they had reached the bus stop where they both got off, they had to say goodbye.

And then Mr. Jenkins remembered his dream and determined to forget about his mid-day dinner one day and take a walk round the building and really see what was going on. But somehow something always prevented him from doing this, and the day when he at last set himself for the job, Mr. Oliver Cromwell Jones swooped on him like a hawk on a field mouse.

'Ah, Mr. Jenkins' he rasped, 'you are just the man I wanted to see.'

And though there was always a fear at the back of his mind that Mr. Oliver Cromwell Jones would find out about his age, he got boldly into the lift. Mr. Oliver Cromwell Jones seemed to take up all the room, and Mr. Jenkins feared that he would have to walk up the stairs. But they managed somehow and were soon on the second floor. Mr. Oliver Cromwell Jones got out of the lift and turned to the left.

Now the pepperpot office was to the right, or so Mr. Jenkins thought, so he called to Mr. Oliver Cromwell Jones and told him that he was going the wrong way.

Mr. Oliver Cromwell Jones turned and looked at him coldly.

'Mr. Jenkins,' he said, 'I do know this building, I have worked here since I was a boy. If you open the door at that end of the corridor where you suggest I should go, I should fall out into the street. So please don't let me have any more of your Monmouthshire jokes, but open the proper door for me quickly.'

Mr. Jenkins obeyed. To his astonishment the key fitted the lock and there inside was the pepperpot office, only with a difference. This office had no pictures on the walls, a very threadbare carpet, and a very uncomfortable chair. In fact it was just the sort of office that you would have expected Mr. Oliver Cromwell Jones to provide. And yet, there on the desk were his papers and figures just as he had left them.

Mr. Oliver Cromwell Jones, looking at him very strangely, said:

'Have you by any chance been drinking?'

*   *   *

And from that moment Mr. Jenkins's confidence went. He was back on the old footing with Mr. Oliver Cromwell Jones who now began to find fault with everything he did. He was accused of being slow, and it was even threatened that if he did not smarten up his ideas his job would be given to somebody else, somebody younger, and Mr. Jenkins feared this more than anything else. Immediately after his holiday he had gone to see the house agent and had paid a deposit on the cottage at Llanwit Major that he had always wanted. He had explained to the man that now he had this new and better paid job in the pepperpot office he would be able to pay the money in regularly. Then he had filled in a form and given his age—this time, correctly.

He had by now given up trying to find the office with the pictures and the view. Always when he tried to go to the old door there was someone in the passage. One day Dillwyn, the boy from Aberdare with the black crinkly hair and the big smile, had asked him if he were going to jump into the street. He began, at last, to feel that he had been dreaming, and that the first pepperpot office was not there, and only existed in his imagination.

November dragged on and it was cold and foggy, and Dilys seemed to be thinner and more frail than ever, and Mr. Jenkins seemed to be making far more mistakes and getting more and more tired and short-sighted.

Then one awful morning Mr. Oliver Cromwell Jones sent for him. Trembling, he got into the wobbly lift and pulled himself up to the big office.

Mr. Oliver Cromwell Jones was sitting huddled in his chair, more than ever like a buzzard on the Llanberis Pass.

At first he appeared not to notice Mr. Jenkins. Then he slowly lifted his head and took his glasses off his beak-like nose. His eyes were like cold grey pebbles left by the tide on a wintry shore.

'It would appear, Mr. Jenkins,' he said quietly, 'that I have placed my trust in the wrong person. The work that you are doing now which started off so well is quite impossible. So inaccurate in fact that it will all have to be done again. I have no option but to send you back to your old job. And if you do not pull up your socks there. . . I am afraid we may have to say goodbye to you altogether.' And Mr. Oliver Cromwell Jones laughed, a hollow croaking laugh like a jackdaw in a ruined tower.

Mr. Jenkins was desperate. He went up to the big desk and holding on to it tightly, spoke directly into the cold pebble eyes of Mr. Oliver Cromwell Jones.

'Mr. Oliver Cromwell Jones, please give me another chance. Please let me put right the things that I have done wrong. My little grand-daughter has been very poorly, and I have been so worried. I know that it should not have affected my work, but it has. Let me try to prove to you that I can indeed do the job that you so kindly gave me. You are a father yourself, extend to me your pity, I need this extra money so much.'

Poor little Mr. Jenkins was moved to tears, and it would indeed have moved anyone who had not a heart of stone.

But it did not move Mr. Oliver Cromwell Jones.

He stood up.

'I am not a hard man,' he said, his face turned yellow by the light from the stained glass, 'but I cannot avoid doing this: this order comes from higher up,' and he pointed to the glass dome as though some important person were sitting up there out in the cold November air. 'I am sorry but you must go back to your office and give over your papers to Mr. Dillwyn Morgan.'

And Mr. Jenkins, tears streaming down his face, went back into the lift. This then was the end of his hopes and the end of his dream of the house with a little bit of land in the Vale of Glamorgan.

He would not know how to tell Dilys.

He got out of the lift and walked sadly towards the pepperpot office. And in his distress he had walked to the right and not to the left. He put the key in the door and there once again was the first office with the pictures on the wall, the posh carpet and the comfortable swivel chair.

And there, better still, lying on top of the desk, was the report. The report that had caused all the trouble, and got him the sack. Only he knew before he picked it up that this time it would be all right. He glanced quickly through it and then rushed back to the lift. He had to wait a few moments before it came, and these moments seemed like years.

At last he reached Mr. Oliver Cromwell Jones's dreaded door. He rushed in and luckily only had to face the secretary.

'Here is the report,' he gasped, 'I must have sent in the wrong one.'

The secretary looked at him and then looked at the papers. She was a kind woman and had a soft spot for Mr. Jenkins.

'I had better give this to Mr. Oliver Cromwell Jones

right away,' she said, 'you are in real hot water and this may save you.'

And it did. And Mr. Jenkins kept his job and went daily to the pepperpot office.

But he always made sure that no one saw him go and walk down the corridor and turn the key and sit at the desk looking out of the window towards the mountains and valleys.

Because to everyone else the pepperpot office did not exist . . .

Soon it was Christmas and Mr. Jenkins was getting on so well with payments on the house that he almost hoped to be in by Easter. He always knelt and said his prayers night and morning as his mother had taught him to do and included in them a plea that the pepperpot office would not again disappear before he had managed to earn the money to get Dilys to the country.

And all went smoothly until one terrible morning when he got to the red brick building, went up the stairs and found that workmen had arrived and that there were ladders and scaffolding blocking the way to the doors where he usually worked. There was nothing for it but to go the other way.

The moment he set foot in the other office, he knew that everything would go wrong. Instead of finding that the work and the adding up and the reports had done themselves overnight, he found that he could do nothing right and that everything was always different, and that no columns of figures seemed to add up the same twice.

Naturally, he came up again before Mr. Oliver Cromwell Jones. It was what might be called a final warning.

Then something worse happened. The people who were selling the cottage to Mr. Jenkins wrote to Mr. Oliver Cromwell Jones for a reference. They had sent him a form to sign.

Now Mr. Oliver Cromwell Jones never signed anything unless he had read every word that was on the paper, even all the tiny print on the back, and therefore it did not take him long to discover that Mr. Jenkins had written his age down as sixty-one.

Mr. Oliver Cromwell Jones sent for his secretary and then sent for poor little Mr. Jenkins.

He was expecting to be sent for anyway as he felt sure that the last sums and figures that he had sent in would be wrong, his luck being out since the disappearance of his pepperpot office.

He got out of the lift and faced Mr. Oliver Cromwell Jones hopelessly.

'I expect you think that I have got you up here to complain about your work as usual,' Mr. Oliver Cromwell Jones said, smiling like a large black cat about to seize a tasty little mouse.

Mr. Jenkins did not answer.

'You would be wrong, though. This time it is a little question of your age.'

Mr. Jenkins shrank deeper inside his worn brown suit.

'How old are you?' said Mr. Oliver Cromwell Jones, looking at the paper he had not yet signed.

Mr. Jenkins thought quickly.

'Fifty-three,' he lied.

'I see,' said Mr. Oliver Cromwell Jones, 'then why have you given your age on this form as sixty-one?'

That was it, thought Mr. Jenkins. Your sins would always find you out, and this was the way God punished you for telling lies.

'I think I shall have to check up on this, and if we find out that you have given some false information, it will be very serious for you indeed.'

There was no answer to this. Mr. Oliver Cromwell Jones had only got to go and look in the Parish register in the church in the Monmouthshire valley, with wisteria growing all over the porch to know that he, Isaac Thomas Jenkins, was lying, and that he was too old to be employed in the red brick building anyway.

He got back into the lift. He thought that the only thing to do would be to run away. Away from the red brick building and the foggy damp air of the city, and above all, away from Mr. Oliver Cromwell Jones. But he knew there was no escape because of Dilys. For if he lost his job and had no longer enough money to look after her, they would put her away in a home where they would only allow him to see her twice a week, which would break both his heart and hers.

And as he was thinking these sad thoughts he got out of the lift and turned right towards his old friend the pepperpot office. He fumbled with the key and opened the door, and there it was again, with the last rays of the February sun shining red through the windows.

He sat down at the desk that he knew would soon no longer be his. He began to pick up the papers, putting them in the files ready for young Dillwyn Aberdare Morgan to take over. Then opening his shabby old suitcase he put away the few things that really belonged to him.

And there, to his great astonishment, he found his birth certificate. At first he was going to put it away quickly for fear of Mr. Oliver Cromwell Jones walking in. Then he had a look at it.

It said that he had been born in Maypole in Monmouthshire.

It said that he was the elder son of Mary and Zacharias Jenkins.

But it also said that he had been born eight years later than he really had.

He sat looking at the piece of paper until the sun had disappeared behind the Caerphilly mountain.

Then he put out the light.

He walked to the door of the pepperpot office and looked out. There was no one about and the corridor looked the same as usual. He wondered if his luck would hold and if the paper would say the same in Mr. Oliver Cromwell Jones' office as it did here.

Liars do not deserve mercy, he knew, but he bravely walked to the lift and rang the bell.

The lift seemed to shoot up more quickly than usual. In fact Mr. Jenkins was in the big office before he had time to collect his wits. He saw too late that he was walking in on something that no one in the red brick building should have been allowed to see.

He saw the great Mr. Oliver Cromwell Jones standing with his shoulders hunched facing a very tall man.

The man had his back to Mr. Jenkins, so he could not see his face. But he could hear his voice and it was very angry.

'So you are going to dismiss this man?' said the voice, 'dismiss him without consulting me?' the voice went on without giving Mr. Oliver Cromwell Jones a chance to answer.

'Dismiss a man who has given the company years of service and who lately has been doing a very difficult job very well? How many times have I told you that I do not approve of these methods?'

And by now poor little Mr. Jenkins knew that they were talking about him. He turned to go back into the lift, but Mr. Oliver Cromwell Jones had seen him.

'The man is here,' he said in a voice that Mr. Jenkins did not recognise, so quiet and humble it seemed.

'He gave a false age, at least I think he did. He is actually sixty-one, and therefore past retiring age. We are searching for his birth certificate.'

Mr. Jenkins stepped forward so that he stood under the stained glass roof.

'I have found the certificate, Mr. Oliver Cromwell Jones,' he said, 'it was with my papers in my office.'

Then he walked bravely across the floor and handed the paper over the desk. Then without looking at the tall man he tiptoed back to the lift. It was time to go home now.

Next day he went to the red brick building to collect his things. He knew that by now Dillwyn Morgan would have replaced him.

But instead he found that someone had replaced Mr. Oliver Cromwell Jones. He, Isaac Jenkins, had got the job.

And though he never saw the pepperpot office again, he often went to look for it, for he knew that he had it to thank for his good fortune and for the fact that he was now able to afford to buy the cottage near Llanwit Major for himself and Dilys. And in the good sea air the little girl grew stronger daily and was soon able to go to school like other children.

And Mr. Jenkins went on saving his money, and when he had enough he built himself a greenhouse from some old window frames from a demolished mansion. He tried to make it look as much like the pepperpot office as possible and there he grew tomatoes and geraniums and cucumbers. And in the good air of the Vale of Glamorgan he and his grand-daughter lived happily ever after.

IORWERTH AND THE PET LAMB

Iorwerth Williams lived with his parents in a stone farmhouse on the old road to the mountain quarry.

The house faced down the valley and seemed to have turned its back on the mountain to protect itself, as well it might, for the mountain conjured up sudden storms and squalls of rain and fierce hail out of a clear sky. In fact, it could not be trusted at all.

'That mountain,' said Iorwerth's father, calling it by the name on the map and shaking his fist, 'it brings us all that bad weather so that I cannot cart in my hay. One day we will all go down into the valley and live in a quieter place away from all these storms.' But Iorwerth didn't take any notice of this because his father had been saying the same thing now for the last ten years and they had never moved. And anyway, everyone forgave the mountain in the summer months before they cut the hay, when it lay there sleeping, far away and blue, and as comfortable-looking as an armchair.

In this part of the country the winters are particularly hard, and Iorwerth's father and mother always had a very bad time with the sheep, digging them out of the snowdrifts in the steep fields, where the poor things were huddled together for warmth in the lee of the high stone walls.

One cold spring evening, Iorwerth's father came into the kitchen of their house and brought with him a tiny lamb. It was so weak it could not stand, and it made a tiny pathetic sound.

'I am afraid he has come too early, and his poor Mam won't last till morning,' said Bob Williams. 'Better keep the little chap warm by the fire.'

So Iorwerth's Mam, who was a very jolly person, went and got a feeding bottle and an old coat, and tried to comfort the poor wee thing. Iorwerth, however, was delighted. Idwal Cwmpenanner, who lived across the other side of the bog on the road to the lake, had had a pet lamb for two years, and now it was a large stout sheep and followed him about like a dog and he called it 'Lana,' after a lady he had seen on the pictures on Saturday night in Bala.

Iorwerth had always wanted an animal of his own. The cat belonged in the cowhouse, and the two sheep dogs, Fly and Mot, lived outside in a shed, and though they were friendly enough, really seemed to belong to his father. Perhaps he would now be able to look after and love this lamb.

Next morning Bob came into the kitchen and said that the ewe had died, and so Iorwerth offered to look after the poor orphan.

'Well, that will be a good thing indeed,' said his Mam. 'The lambs will soon be arriving so fast that your dad and I will be too busy in the fields to see to him.'

So Iorwerth gave the lamb its bottle and called it Arthur, after a king the teacher had taught him about in school. And indeed the lamb would have followed the boy there every morning had he been allowed, but he was shut in the kitchen and used to wait at the gate for his return. Sometimes he followed Iorwerth about bleating quietly, but sometimes, when he was thirsty, he would make a terribly loud noise, and Iorwerth's Mam would chase him out of the kitchen.

The weather grew better, and the white waterfalls that had run down the face of the mountain like milk gradually disappeared. Iorwerth used to go out with his fishing rod and catch a few small trout for breakfast, and Arthur was always there too, nibbling the thin grass on the rocky banks of the stream.

Iorwerth was blissfully happy, and did not notice that Arthur was growing from a spindly-legged pretty lamb into a rather fat and plain sheep. The days lengthened and the fields grew bright with the flowers that they called hay in these parts. Dog daisies, scabious, yellow lady's slipper, buttercups and blue birds' eye speedwell. The sheep were turned into the mountain pastures, and Arthur went with them. Yet he was not like the other sheep at all because he was not frightened of the dogs and didn't rush over and stand with the rest of the flock. Indeed, he would sometimes come down into the yard and play games with the dogs, butting them with the small horns he was now growing. And whenever he heard Iorwerth walking, whistling up the road, he would stop eating, lift his head, and give a loud bleat, and as often as not would trot down into the road and join his master.

And though he was fat and woolly, and had a silly, kind face, and eyes like grey marbles, Iorwerth loved him with his whole heart, and thought he was the most beautiful lamb in the world.

Soon it was time for the dipping, and the sheep were driven off the mountains. And the men from the neighbouring farms came and helped. Iorwerth's Mam had made lots of lovely cakes and seemed to be bustling about cutting bread and butter all day. And

Fly and Mot worked all day too, obeying their master's whistle and careering off until they were just specks on the mountainside, rounding up the silly, frightened sheep.

It was a lovely sunny day, but the mountain looked very black and close, almost as though it were in Mrs. Williams's back garden, so everybody knew it was up to something.

'They're all down now,' said Iorwerth's father.

'No, Dad, I can still see one up there, on a ledge above the lake,' said the boy.

'Annwyl, what eyes you've got, my boy,' said his father. 'Why, so there is.' And he whistled to Fly, and she hurtled off, quicker than thought, far away and up into the dark recesses of the mountain. She seemed to reach the sheep in no time, and Iorwerth's father whistled again and, though it was quite a way off, the sound carried perfectly on the still air.

Fly lay flat on her stomach and crawled towards the sheep. She had been taught to do this so as not to frighten them, and was clever enough to see that the sheep was standing on a ledge and did not wish it to fall over into the lake. Nearer and nearer Fly crawled, but the sheep did not move.

'What's the matter with it? It does not seem to mind the dog. Where is your lamb?' and he turned to see his son's anxious face.

'Whistle the dog, Dad; tell her to come back. I'll

get Arthur off that ledge. He'll come if he knows I want him. What can he be doing up there anyway?' And he ran off through the heather and bilberries up towards the shores of the cold little lake that lay cradled in the mountain.

So Bob Williams whistled Fly back, and she rushed past Iorwerth without so much as wagging her tail, so intent was she on obeying her master's orders.

Iorwerth started to climb the steep side of the lake. He called: 'Come on, Arthur, cariad bach, come on.'

But Arthur didn't take any notice, and started to nibble the grass. So Iorwerth went on scrambling up, and soon was level with Arthur, and called again, and the lamb, or ram as indeed he now was, looked at him but did not move. So Iorwerth went crabwise across the face of the mountain calling 'Arthur' with what breath he had left.

And just at that moment, the mountain played one of its tricks. It had quite a number of tricks, but the nastiest was suddenly, and without any warning at all, to cover itself all over with a light mist: Iorwerth suddenly realised what the mountain was up to, and scrambled as fast as he could on to the ledge. By the time he had got there, the mist was down, and he and the ram were alone in a cold white space, with no trace of the lake, and the mountain face shelving dangerously away beneath them.

'Come, cariad,' he said, and the lamb looked up

79

and bleated and turned deliberately away from the boy
and started to walk off the ledge. Now this made
Iorwerth very frightened because he knew that this
side of the mountain was really steep, and he doubted
whether there would be any foothold for him or his
pet. But follow he must, for whatever lay ahead in the
white unknown, he must not let the lamb face it alone.

He braced himself on the ledge and called. The
sheep bleated and he followed the sound. Mirac-
ulously there seemed to be a little sheep's path among
the scree and loose stones, and Iorwerth was able to
walk one foot in front of the other as though he were
on a tight rope. He could just see Arthur, but could not
touch him as the sheep kept climbing on. Then a great
rock loomed out of the mist and the path zig-zagged
round it and on and still up.

Iorwerth stopped for breath and the lamb stopped
too and called, and as the boy didn't answer, he called
again as though he were anxious for the child to
follow, almost as though he had something to show
him.

It was strange and cold and quiet on the mountain,
and Iorwerth had no idea of the time, and wondered if
his mother would be making tea and worrying about
him. He ought to turn back, he supposed, but somehow
he couldn't.

Then he realised that the sheep track had widened
and looked like one of those cart roads that the men

used for collecting the peat off the mountain. But it puzzled him, for he did not remember such a track so high up, and he thought he knew this bad old mountain well. Where, then, was his friend, his Arthur, leading him?

Then he looked up and saw a great wall piled up amongst the crags. It might have been a sheep wall, but somehow it didn't look like one. And then the peat tracks widened and became a road. Iorwerth was lost, bewildered, amazed, but though it was starting to get dark, he was not frightened because the sheep was still leading him on and calling as he went. Suddenly out of the mist ahead shone a light. Iorwerth saw that the wall on his left came down to meet the wall on his right, and joining the two was a gatehouse with a great closed gate. And from one of the windows of his gatehouse steamed a welcoming, golden light.

And faintly, as from far away, Iorwerth could hear the sound of music.

Then Arthur, this extraordinary pet lamb, walked up to the great gate, bleated and stopped. And Iorwerth stood beside him, his hand on the sheep's springy wool. He was just wondering what would happen next when suddenly the great door swung silently open and the music became louder and more glorious. It was singing, too, and sounded like a choir. Iorwerth was very excited. They seemed to be in the courtyard of a large old plas, and the windows of a huge room opposite glowed with brilliant light in all the rainbow colours of stained glass.

The sheep looked up at the boy and trotted across the courtyard; as he did so a door opened in the mansion, and the sound of many glorious voices singing poured into the dark, misty evening. Iorwerth was unafraid, and followed the lamb into the hall. He had never heard such singing; it was better than any of the choirs in the Eisteddfod. He reckoned they must sing like that in heaven. There they stood, hundreds and hundreds of them, basses, tenors, contraltos and sopranos, all dressed in cloth of gold, with a wonderful look of great happiness on their faces, singing away like mad. And there were men with banners blowing long trumpets and harps and flutes and lots of other musical instruments that Iorwerth didn't recognise but had heard on the wireless. It was very warm inside this glittering hall, and a man came and gave Iorwerth a lovely gold plate covered with cakes and some sweet tea in a gold goblet.

The singing reached its climax and suddenly died, and into the midst of the throng of singers stepped a small figure. She bowed to someone sitting behind Iorwerth and turned to the harpist. Then she smiled and started to sing, and Iorwerth suddenly realised that this was the most beautiful girl he had ever seen, and that she was singing in her lovely treble voice the most lovely air he had ever heard. It was a song about a stream full of brown trout and somewhere, under a rock, buried treasure for the boy that could walk with his true love to the gate on the bridge at the new moon. The voice soared and fell, and soon the whole choir took up the song and Iorwerth closed his eyes as the music flooded over him.

And when he woke, he found that it was bright sunlight, and that he had been asleep in a corner of rocks on the mountain with Arthur standing patiently beside him. The mist had all gone, and he made his way easily down to the farmhouse. It seemed to be still only tea time, and his Mam kissed him and told him to wash his hands under the tap. His father came in with the dogs and said, 'Well, Iorwerth boy, I thought we'd lost you both in that mist!' and Iorwerth did not know what to say, as he was already beginning to be a bit hazy about what had happened. So he called Arthur, who was playing a silly sheep's game with the dogs. Then they picked him up, for though he was really a very wonderful sheep, he still had to go and be dipped like the others.

'Weren't you frightened up there, all alone?' said his father. 'I was once lost in a mist up there and . . .' and just as Iorwerth hoped his father was going to tell him something wonderful, one of the men called him, and the sentence lay unfinished between them. And then they all sat down to tea and bread and butter and jam and some lovely soda cake that his Mam had baked.

And Arthur grew up to be a fine ram and the father of his flock. And Iorwerth never mentioned his strange adventure to anyone, not even to his Dad. He often went up the mountain to try and find the mansion, but he never seemed to be able to find the sheep's track or the road.

Then, one night five years later, when Iorwerth was seventeen, he went down to Bala by the big lake to a Test Concert.

People had come from miles all over the country, from sheep farms and lonely places on the mountains, to compete and sing. They did not all sing well, but they all put their whole hearts into it, and sang very loudly. It was very hot and smokey in the hall, and Iorwerth was beginning to feel sleepy when suddenly a young girl in the under twenty's solo started to sing a Welsh ballad that several other people had sung. But something about her voice froze Iorwerth to his seat. Where had he heard that voice before? It was so beautiful and clear, and she stood there as though she were singing in a dream. Iorwerth left the hall after her song because he felt he couldn't bear to hear any other voices after hers. Standing outside in the street was his friend, Idwal, from Cwmpenanner.

'Want a lift?' said Idwal kindly, slapping him on the back. 'I'm just waiting for Mair.'

'Mair?' said Iorwerth hazily.

'Yes, you know,' said Idwal. 'That girl who's just

84

sung; she's staying with us; she's my mother's sister's husband's niece.'

Iorwerth stepped like a man in a dream into the back of Idwal's old car and sat down amongst the pieces of the secondhand electric light machine that Idwal had bought at the market. Happily there was no front seat in the old car, so he would have to sit next to Mair, and, anyway, Idwal's pet lamb, Lana, always stood there by her master.

Mair got into the car and sat down beside Iorwerth on the broken springs. He looked at her and knew at once that she was, for him, the most beautiful girl in the world.

They drove noisily out of the town and up the steep hill, where the birches grow, on and up the old road to the mountain.

'You sang beautifully . . . beautifully . . .' Iorwerth said at last.

'Thank you,' said Mair, humbly.

'I want to hear you sing again and again,' said the trembling Iorwerth. 'I want to hear you sing "Llwyn Onn" and "Tros y Garreg" and the song about buried treasure and the brown trout under the rock and the lovers on the bridge in the new moon . . .' He stopped suddenly, fearful at what he was saying.

And Mair started to sing. . .

And as her voice soared through the night, Iorwerth

was once again in the mist and the mighty magic mansion on the mountain.

It was the same voice, the same song. . . Where, or where had she come from . . .?

The wonderful voice ceased, and the old car pulled up with a jolt.

'Here you are, man; goodnight and sleep well,' said Idwal.

'Thank you,' said Iorwerth, still dreaming. 'Where did you learn that song?'

'It's an old song,' said Mair lightly.

'I've heard it before, on that mountain,' he said.

She looked at him strangely and said goodnight. And before he had time to say more, Idwal drove noisily off up the road, and she was gone.

And Iorwerth, his heart pounding, looked up into the glowing sky and saw the new moon. And he went over to Arthur's shed and the ram called. And Iorwerth said, 'To-morrow, Arthur, we will go to Cwmpenanner. . .'

THE POST OFFICE BADGER

Mrs. Morgan kept the little post office at the end of the valley. She sold groceries and sweets and was licenced to sell tobacco. She was a widow, having buried her husband some four years before all this happened. She was a very kind person and much loved and respected by her friends, neighbours and the travellers who passed along the main road.

The small road that went up the valley past the post office looked as though it were going somewhere important, for it was fairly wide and seemed to have a good tarred surface. But all it really did was to twist and turn up the valley following the river, go through several gates, getting rougher and rougher, and finally end up as a cart track leading into the great wastes of the boggy sheepwalk. And all the roads around leading off the main road seemed to do the same thing, winding on and up past farms and barns, then losing courage and dwindling away to nothing in the great lonely spaces of the Cambrian Mountains.

And many farm people seemed to have left these valleys when the cattle trade went, and all around were roofless houses with elder bushes sprouting in the roofs and chimneys, and nettles and brambles where the barns had stood and the cattle had been housed.

Mrs. Morgan had been born in this district, and though now she was certainly a bit lonely, nothing would persuade her to go and live with her daughter in London. She loved the sweet damp air, the peaceful far cries of the sheep, the curlews and the moorhens, and nowhere else she declared could you make a decent cup of tea like she brewed with the soft strong water.

She had the wireless, and when the electric came her daughter had promised to give her a television.

One Thursday afternoon in November, it being early closing, Mrs. Morgan had shut the shop and gone for a walk up the valley to get a few sticks and to see if there were still some late blackberries. But though it had been a fine sharp day, it was brewing up for rain now and she turned back sooner than she intended, drew the curtains to shut out the storm, lit the lamps and put the kettle on for tea. And she was just settling down in front of the fire when she heard a snuffling and scraping at the back door.

Thinking it would be Hopkin Pugh's pig got out as usual, she peeped through the window, hoping that it was not trampling down her few currant bushes or rooting up her newly sprouted broad beans.

As she couldn't see anything at the door, she made the tea and buttered some Welsh cakes. And just as she did this the snuffling and scraping started again, only this time at the front door.

Mrs. Morgan got up, unbolted the door and looked outside. Though it was by now quite dark, she could just see a large badger standing a little way back from the threshold. It was staring at her, watching to see if she would shut the door.

Mrs. Morgan's first instinct was to say 'Shoo' and hope that it would go away, but there was something so hopeful about the way that it was standing there that she stepped aside and it walked straight into her kitchen, and before she knew where she was it was sitting in front of her fire for all the world as though it had lived there all its life.

At first she did not know what to do, so she went on with her tea, and then thinking that it might be thirsty, she offered it some rice pudding that was left over from her dinner.

It seemed to like this so she went out and got it some more milk, then she stepped over it and put some wood on the fire and it looked up at her as though to say thank you, then rolled over and went to sleep.

Mrs. Morgan wanted to put the wireless on to hear the news, but she did not want to disturb her new friend, for that was how she already felt about the badger. So instead she took her reading glasses off the the kitchen shelf and got out of the cupboard an old natural history book she had had as a child.

She turned to BADGER and read a short paragraph.

They did not do much harm, it said, and they were very often blamed for the thievings and killings that had been done by a fox. They were hunted and cruelly treated for this reason and their fur was used frequently for making gentlemen's shaving brushes.

Mrs. Morgan shut the book. How dreadful, she thought, and looked down at the snoring badger. What if some of the boys were to come home late from market and see the poor creature lying there? And how long was it going to stay, she wondered.

And so fearing to disturb it she sat quietly knitting all evening, missing her favourite programme on the wireless.

Then she lit a candle and crept up early to bed.

Towards dawn she heard the badger snorting and

grunting again, and she went downstairs to find it standing at the back door waiting to get out. As she opened the back door it looked up at her again as if to say thank you, and trotted out into the night.

And that, thought Mrs. Morgan sadly, is the end of that.

But she was wrong, for just at the same time the next evening it came back, and the next evening, and the next, so that she decided to open the cupboard door under the stairs and put an empty Player's cigarette carton filled with straw for it to sleep in.

For many nights she was very happy with this arrangement. She sat by the fire knitting socks for her young nephew and playing the wireless very quietly, while her new friend lay in the cigarette carton, its funny black and white striped head hanging over the side of the box.

She wished she knew if it were a sow or a boar, because she wanted to give it a name. And so she decided to call it Stripes, which name she felt would do for either.

Then one night Tegwyn Cwm Uchaf banged on the door and asked for some fags.

Mrs. Morgan put a screen up to hide Stripes, and opened the front door a very little way. She liked Tegwyn and in the ordinary way would have been very glad to have a chat with him, but now she feared what might happen if he saw the badger.

'Rough night, Mrs. Morgan,' said Tegwyn, 'it's blowing up for a real storm. And Hopkin Pugh is blowing up for a storm too. His pig is out as usual, and the ram has got too early with the sheep and something has stolen a lot of his hens.'

'Fox probably,' said Mrs. Morgan very quickly.

'Or badger perhaps,' said Tegwyn. 'Anyway, whatever it is, Hopkin says he will catch it in his trap.'

Mrs. Morgan shuddered. 'Would you like a cup of tea, Tegwyn?' she asked. 'Warm you up a bit before you go up the mountain.'

But Tegwyn said he had to go, his old mare was fretting outside and he had a long wet ride ahead of him.

As she heard him trot away into the stormy night, Mrs. Morgan took away the screen that was hiding Stripes. The animal looked up at her intently as though it wanted something. More rice pudding perhaps, she thought, and went into the kitchen to get some.

The badger was very pleased with this and got out of his cigarette carton and sat by the fire.

Then Mrs. Morgan spoke to him.

'Stripes,' she said, 'I do not know what you do with yourself when you are away from here, and really it is not for me to ask, but I hope you don't go near any chickens, particularly any belonging to Hopkin Pugh.'

Then she turned up the wireless and finished the

toe of a sock. Stripes turned round and looked at her and went back into his box.

Mrs. Morgan worried a lot about Hopkin Pugh. Many times her husband had had words with him for he was always grousing and complaining and swearing, saying that other people's sheep were on his sheep walk and that someone else's cattle had broken down his fences. He was not a bad man really, but altogether changed since the drink had got him. And so she hoped and prayed that he would not come to her door and bang and ask her to sell him cigarettes or tobacco late at night.

Early next morning when she let the badger out as usual, she called after it, 'Now mind, and remember what I told you last night, keep away from Hopkin Pugh's chickens.'

But as the days grew shorter and the lamps had to be lit earlier, Stripes stayed out later and later, and Mrs. Morgan got more and more worried, for she knew that by now Hopkin Pugh would have fattened up that shed full of poor gobbling turkeys and the geese that marched in single file down to the stream, to say nothing of the dozens of cockerels. And Stripes seemed to be getting much fatter. Then one awful day when she was cleaning out his cigarette carton and putting straw in it, she found the bottom full of feathers. That night when Stripes came home she gave him the biggest rice pudding she had ever made, hoping that if he had enough of that he would forget about whatever else he was trying to steal and eat.

Just before Christmas there was a heavy fall of snow. Mrs. Morgan had always liked snow, remembering the happy days at home as a child with her brothers and sisters sliding and skating, making snowmen and snowballing each other and the grown-ups. And now she hoped that if there was a fresh fall in the night she would be able to follow the badger when he left the post office.

So one December evening when the snow was piling up thickly and quietly against the post office windows, and Stripes was snoring away in his cigarette carton she made herself an extra strong cup of tea to keep herself awake, lit a candle and went upstairs. It was just after ten, which was only three hours after he had eaten an enormous rice pudding, that she heard the badger snuffling and scraping to get out.

She carried the candle downstairs and had a good mind not to open the door, but the creature looked up at her so imploringly that as usual her heart melted. She pulled open the door and as Stripes waddled out she noticed that it had stopped snowing and that his tracks were going to be very clear and easy to follow. She shut her eyes and counted a hundred, like she used to do as a child playing hide and seek, then she put on a scarf, snow boots and her nephew's duffle coat which she had kept since the war. She followed the footsteps easily up through the first gate on the road and for a hundred yards or so more. Then they turned off and made for a gap in the hedge. Though it was quite wide enough for a badger to get through, it certainly was not wide enough for Mrs. Morgan; but she knew that on the other side of the hedge there were short scrubby young oak trees, and that if she had to go round by the gate she would lose the tracks. So she threw her head scarf over the hedge to mark the place and walked on up to the gate.

And at that same moment a large party of men and boys came into view round the bend in the road. They were shouting and singing and carrying lanterns.

Carol party probably, thought Mrs. Morgan, as they came towards her, but why come up this valley? There was only one house occupied and that was at the very top.

But as they got nearer she saw that they were not going out singing and that they carried spades and shovels and guns, and were followed by two snapping terriers. Mrs. Morgan wondered if she should hide, and then realising that that would look foolish she stepped boldly into the road.

Walking in front of the party was Hopkin Pugh.

'Good evening, Mrs. Morgan,' he shouted. 'You're out late for a widow lady, aren't you?'

This was meant to be a joke, but as everybody liked

and respected Mrs. Morgan more than they liked and respected Hopkin Pugh, nobody laughed.

'You're out late too,' she said, not wishing to know why.

'We're out to kill a badger,' he said. 'Two of my geese have gone, fat ones too, and five turkeys and goodness knows how many cockerels.'

Mrs. Morgan felt colder than the snow.

'It must be a fox,' she stammered, 'badgers don't do anything like that. They live off insects and rice pudding.'

'Rice pudding?' said Hopkin Pugh, 'wherever did you get that idea from? Have you seen one around here?'

'No,' lied Mrs. Morgan, 'never.'

'There was one outside your door the other night,' said one of the boys. 'Scratching on it, she was, trying to get in. When she saw my dog she went off.'

'Well, if you haven't seen one before tonight,' Hopkin Pugh said brutally, 'we'll bring you back a dead one and you can have his head put up in the post office. Now go home, cariad, it's too late for ladies to be out alone.'

And he burst into song and they all joined in and went their way up the valley.

Mrs. Morgan waited until they were out of sight and then went and fetched her scarf off the hedge and went sadly home.

There was nothing to do except wait.

And the minutes were like hours, and the hours were like years, until she heard the boys come back. She huddled in her corner by the stove but they did not come in, and they were not singing, and when their lights had disappeared she looked out of the door and saw that it was snowing again, hard. And she went to lock up, and as she did so she heard a quiet grunt, and there standing outside the back door was her dear friend Stripes.

'Oh, cariad, come in,' she cried, but the animal did not move and as she went nearer to it she saw that it was holding one foot up as though injured. She had up to now always been afraid to touch it, but this time she really felt that it needed her and went across to it and gave it a gentle shove so that it trundled into the kitchen. It limped into the cigarette carton and lay down in front of the fire. She rushed quickly and got the rice pudding which she always had ready in the larder, but it turned its head away as though food was the last thing it wanted.

She examined the foot and of course realised that it must have been in a trap, one of Hopkin Pugh's, no doubt. She got some warm water and bathed it and tied it up with a bit of clean butter muslin. Then she turned the lights very low and played some soothing music on the radio.

And just as the B.B.C. announcer was signing off,

there came a knock at the door. Mrs. Morgan did not answer. Whoever had come at this late hour she determined not to let in. But whoever it was went on knocking. Still she did not answer.

'Mrs. Morgan,' called a muffled voice. 'Can you help me? My wife is took bad.'

Mrs. Morgan froze in horror. It was Hopkin Pugh.

'Can I use the telephone?' he called. 'The kiosk is stopped up.'

As the post mistress, Mrs. Morgan knew her duty. She opened the door. Hopkin Pugh struggled in but before he had time to say anything about Stripes, Mrs. Morgan attacked.

'I am going to help you, Hopkin Pugh,' she said, 'provided you leave my friend alone. This beast has been my companion for months now and it has been caught in one of your traps. I know that it cannot have killed or stolen your geese or turkeys because I have given it plenty to eat every day. Good rice pudding, honey and milk. It is my friend, Hopkin Pugh, and I will prove to you that this animal is not the thief. Now you may use the telephone.'

And Hopkin Pugh was so flabbergasted at what he saw and heard that he did meekly what he was told. And Mrs. Morgan made some soup and put it in a billycan and went down with Hopkin Pugh and sat with his poor wife until the doctor came.

Then as she was going, Hopkin Pugh thanked her.

'I've been a bad man, I know,' he said, 'I'll never forget this, though. You have been a true friend. I'll leave that animal alone if you can prove to me that it does not leave your house and garden.'

And Mrs. Morgan went home knowing indeed that this was something that she could not prove.

But for a little while until after Christmas she was safe for the badger had been too much hurt to leave the house for long. But it soon grew better and started to go away for longer.

And on Twelfth Night when the moon was full and all the hills and valleys shining like icing cakes, Stripes stood at the back door, went out and turned to look back at Mrs. Morgan. For the life of her she could not think what he wanted. Then he went a little further, stopped and turned again.

She started to follow and through the frosty night they went, on up the road past the old quarry, on and up until the road lost itself in the boggy mountain side. But still the animal seemed to know its way, and though Mrs. Morgan knew she was getting farther and farther away from home, the fire and the wireless, she still followed. Soon they were making their way up one of the steep valleys which disappeared again into the folds of the hills. A stream ran down this cwm and Mrs. Morgan could hear it and see the steam coming from its sulphury waters. And the badger stopped and drank and Mrs. Morgan thought she heard something bark. She looked up on the hillside above and saw, quite clearly in the moon-light, two foxes, each with a hen in its mouth. She heard more barking and saw that there were four more growling and tearing up a large dead turkey.

Stripes looked at her, but still he went on. By now the path was too steep for the snow to lie and walking was easier. They turned a corner by a large rock and there, gleaming in the moonlight, was a small lake, shallow and placid, edged with reeds, and swimming on the lake were three large, fat, white geese. They seemed not in the least afraid of Stripes: in fact, they came forward eagerly to greet him. Then he waddled off behind the rock and showed Mrs. Morgan where there was the entrance to a small cave. He stood waiting while the geese marched in and then, pushing with his snout, he rolled a stone across the opening.

Then he looked up at her again and they started the long journey home.

Mrs. Morgan and Stripes lived happily together for a long time after that. Hopkin Pugh believed her story about the foxes and he and the boys went out and caught them. But they never found the geese or the cave. And one long late summer night, probably Midsummer Night, Mrs. Morgan went up there and found the geese were still swimming there with a dozen goslings, only this time they flew away when they saw her come, honking and circling around her. Bird watchers came to see the rare wild geese and Hopkin Pugh never knew that they were the children of the fat goose and gander which had been ordered for Mr. James the solicitor's Christmas dinner.

Soon the electric came and Mrs. Morgan did get the television, and she and the badger sat watching it together through many happy evenings.